Sharing a Shell

For Ally – JD

For Jane, Julian and Kai.
Have fun in your new home. – LM

First published 2004 by Macmillan Children's Books
This edition published 2018 by Macmillan Children's Books
an imprint of Pan Macmillan
The Smithson, 6 Briset Street, London EC1M 5NR
Associated companies throughout the world
www.panmacmillan.com

ISBN: 978-1-5098-6270-2

3 5 7 9 8 6 4

A CIP catalogue record for this book is available
from the British Library.

Printed in China.

Sharing a Shell

WRITTEN BY
JULIA DONALDSON

ILLUSTRATED BY
LYDIA MONKS

MACMILLAN CHILDREN'S BOOKS

Look! A crab – a crab with no shell,
Running along by the sea.

Tap, tap, tap!

"You can't come in!
You can't share a shell with me."

Look! A gull, with a wide-open beak.

Run for your life, Crab – hide!

At last, in a pool, an empty shell!
Quick, Crab! Scuttle inside.

One crab, safe in his shell,
Under the summer sun,
Roaming all over the rock pool
In his wonderful home for one.

Look! A blob, a bright purple blob.
What can this blob thing be?
"Go away, Blob, whoever you are –
You can't share a shell with me."

"I'm an anemone, not a blob.
Please let me share your shell.
Give me a ride to look for some food
And perhaps I can help you as well."

Look! A fish, with jaws open wide.
"Fresh crab for dinner – here goes!"

Out shoots a tentacle, quick as a flash,
Stinging the fish on the nose!

Two friends, sharing a shell,
Under a sky of blue,

Romping all over the rock pool
In their wonderful home for two.

Look! A brush thing, trying to get in,
Wiggling and making a fuss.

"Go away, Brush, whoever you are –
You can't share a shell with us."

"I'm not a brush, I'm a bristleworm.
Please let me in – don't be mean.

I love doing housework; I'll suck up the scraps
And keep the shell lovely and clean."

Three friends, sharing a shell,
Down by the sparkling sea,
Rollicking all round the rock pool
In their wonderful home for three.

But look how they've grown! The shell is too small.
"You're getting too heavy," says Crab.
"I'm fed up with being your taxi.
It's time that you found a new cab."

"Really!" says Blob. "How ungrateful!
Here I am, slaving away,
Scaring off all the fierce fishes.
If that's how you feel, I won't stay."

"Peace!" cries Brush, but nobody hears.
The other two creatures split up.
Blob finds an empty ice-cream tub.
Cup finds a nice paper cup.

Crab in the cup, Blob on the tub,
Each one pretends to be glad.
Brush, doing both lots of housework,
Knows they are lonely and sad.

Look! A storm, a terrible storm,
Crashing and flashing all night.
Two homes, smashed on the rocks.
Oh, what a terrible sight!

But, look! A shell, a beautiful shell.
Crab and Anemone stare,
Too shy to speak to each other,
Too proud to say, "Shall we share?"

Listen! A voice! And out pokes a head
From the whelk shell washed up by the foam.
"It's ready. I've done all the housework.
Climb on and come in – whelkome home!"

Three friends, sharing a shell,
Happy as housemates can be,

Rocketing all round the rock pool
In their wonderful home for three!